Also by Matt Madden:

Black Candy
Odds Off
99 Ways to Tell a Story: Exercises in Style

By Matt Madden and Jessica Abel:

Drawing Words and Writing Pictures
Mastering Comics

Design & Production: Matt Madden & Tom Kaczynski

UNCIVILIZED BOOKS
P. O. Box 6534
Minneapolis, MN 55406
USA
uncivilizedbooks.com

First Edition, Oct 2021

10 9 8 7 6 5 4 3 2 1

ISBN 978-1-941250-44-0

DISTRIBUTED TO THE TRADE BY:
Consortium Book Sales & Distribution, LLC.
34 Thirteenth Avenue NE, Suite 101
Minneapolis, MN 55413-1007
cbsd.com
Orders: (800) 283-3572

Printed in China

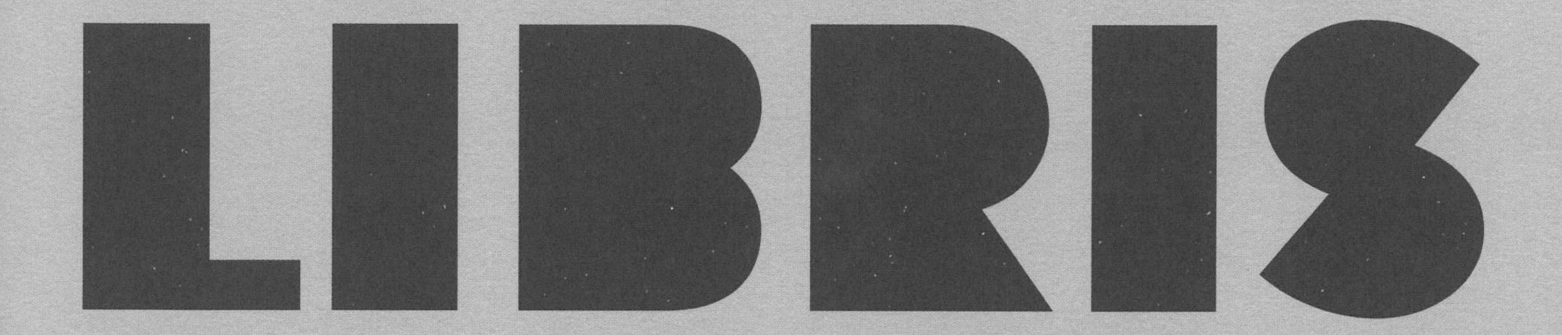

A COMIC BY MATT MADDEN

UNCIVILIZED

CHAPTER ONE

How long have I been standing in this doorway? I steady myself as a wave of vertigo hits me...
The rug seems to float in the air as if superimposed on the rest of the scene in front of me.
I already feel light-headed from the upheaval that brought me here in the first place.

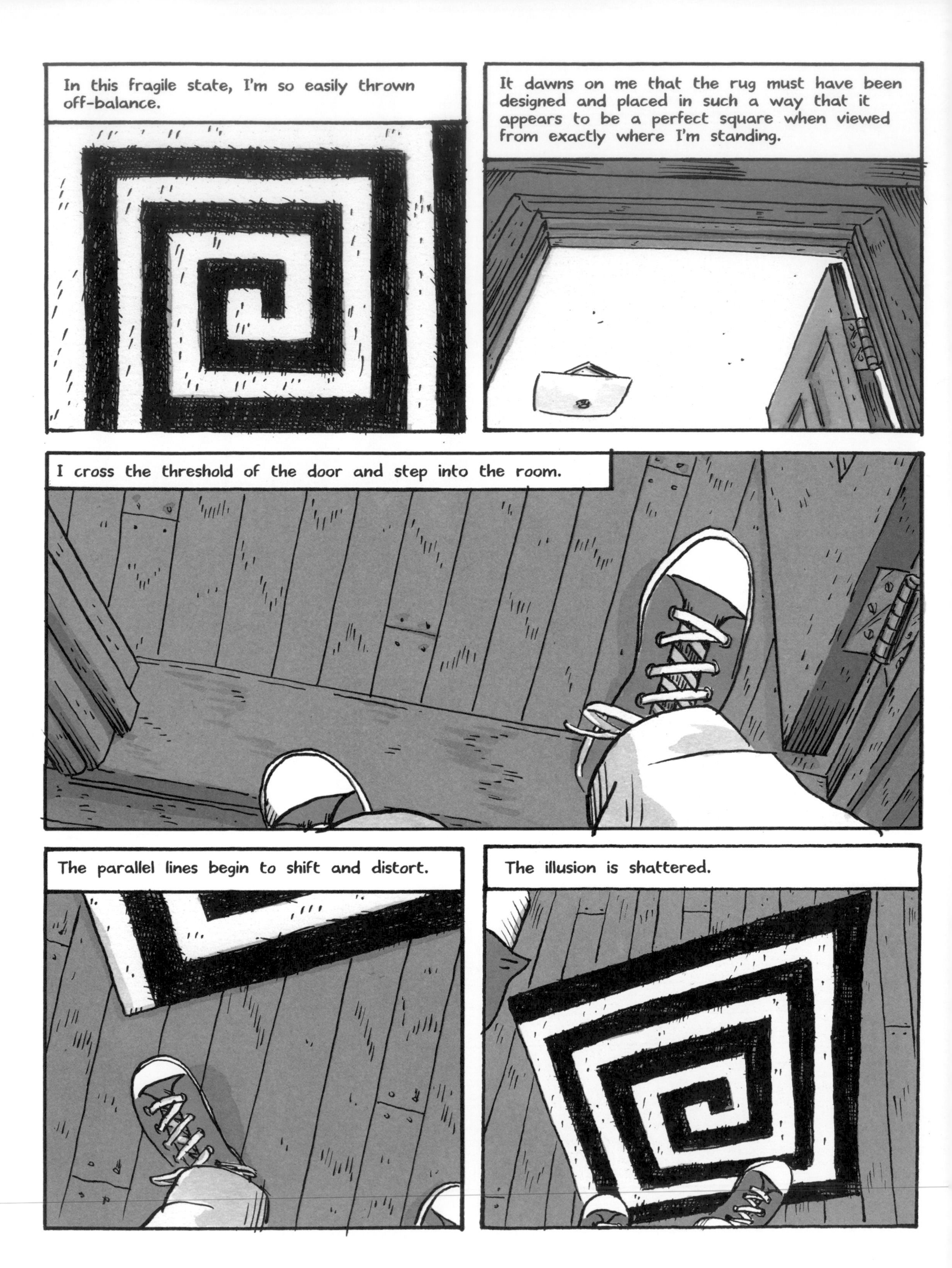
In this fragile state, I'm so easily thrown off-balance.
It dawns on me that the rug must have been designed and placed in such a way that it appears to be a perfect square when viewed from exactly where I'm standing.
I cross the threshold of the door and step into the room.
The parallel lines begin to shift and distort.
The illusion is shattered.

I feel a strange sensation, like I've passed through a funhouse mirror, and now I find myself on the other side of the looking glass.

As the door clicks shut, my past is cut off and I feel a mixture of relief and apprehension...

So, here I am with my duffel bag and a bottle of nice tequila to fortify me as I try to make sense of things.

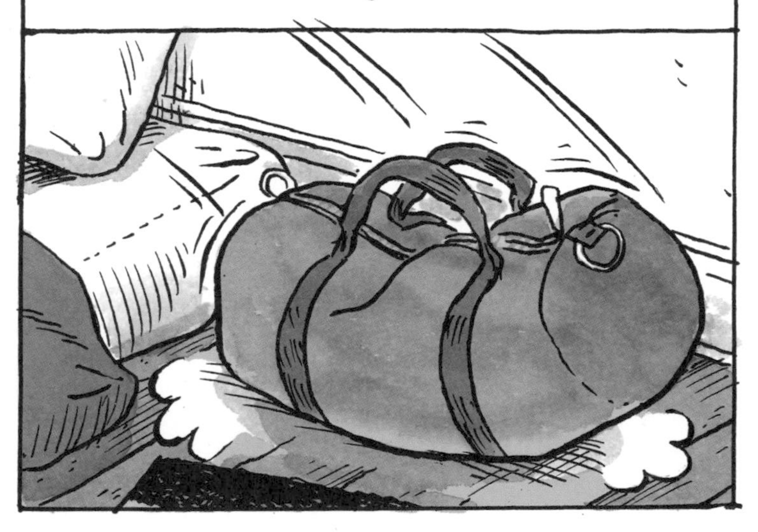

I'm an exile from my own life. I won't bore you with the details but let's just say I practically ended up living in the gutter.

I collapse on the futon and fall asleep, I have no idea for how long.

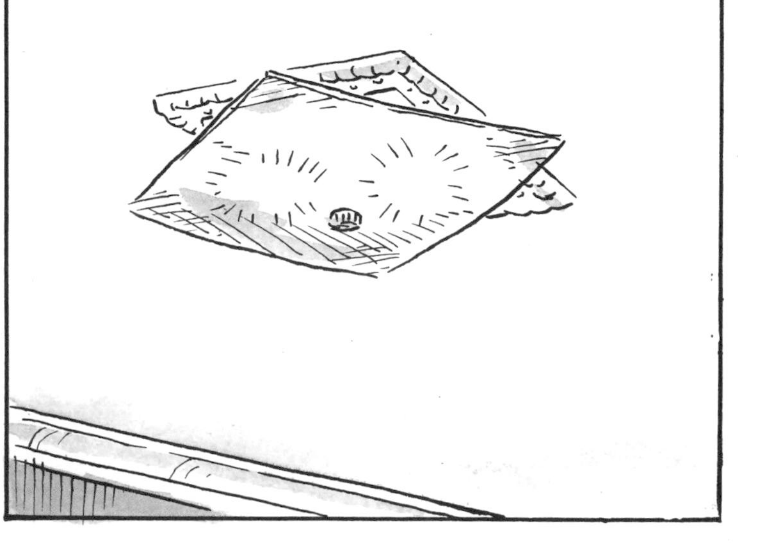

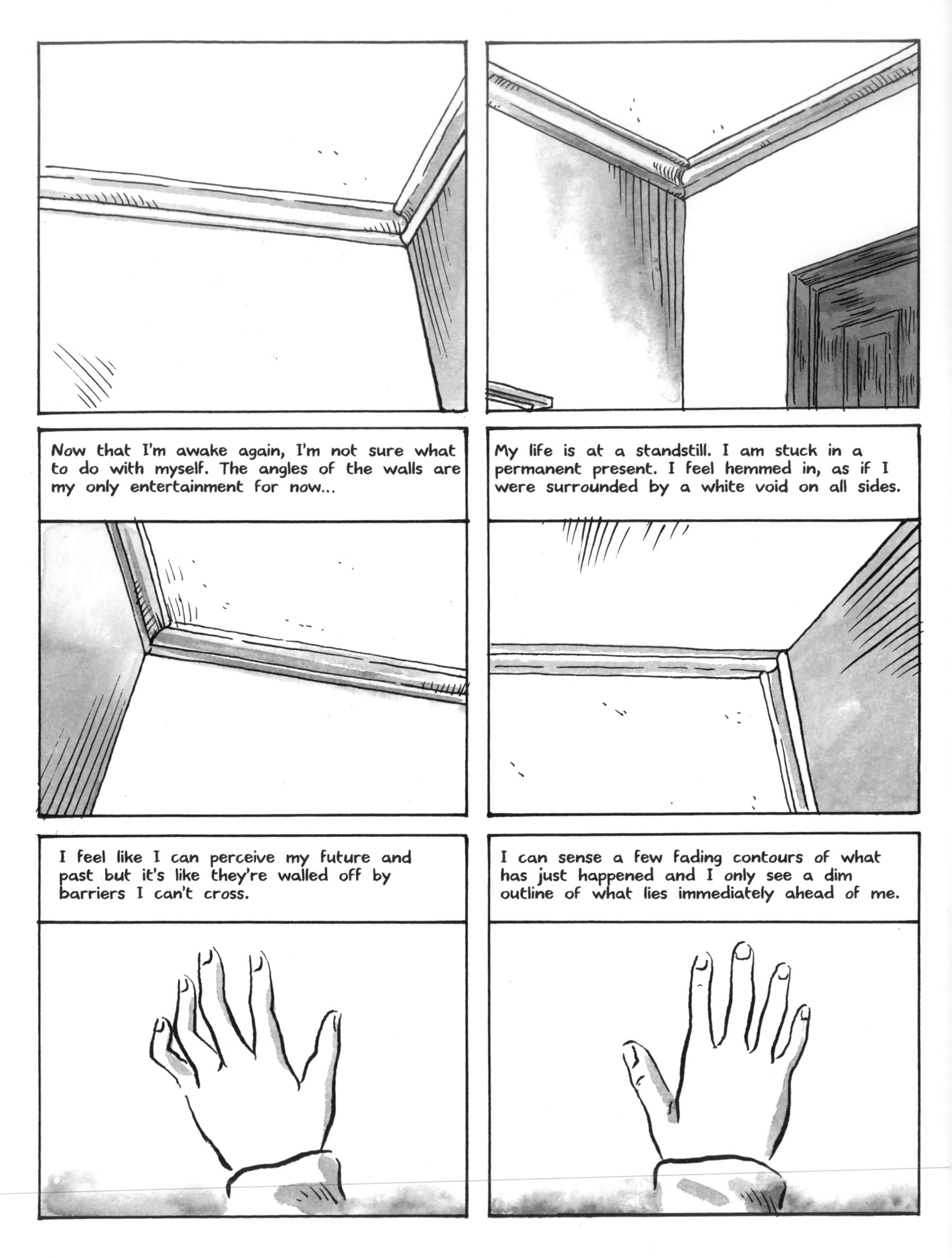
Now that I'm awake again, I'm not sure what to do with myself. The angles of the walls are my only entertainment for now...
My life is at a standstill. I am stuck in a permanent present. I feel hemmed in, as if I were surrounded by a white void on all sides.
I feel like I can perceive my future and past but it's like they're walled off by barriers I can't cross.
I can sense a few fading contours of what has just happened and I only see a dim outline of what lies immediately ahead of me.

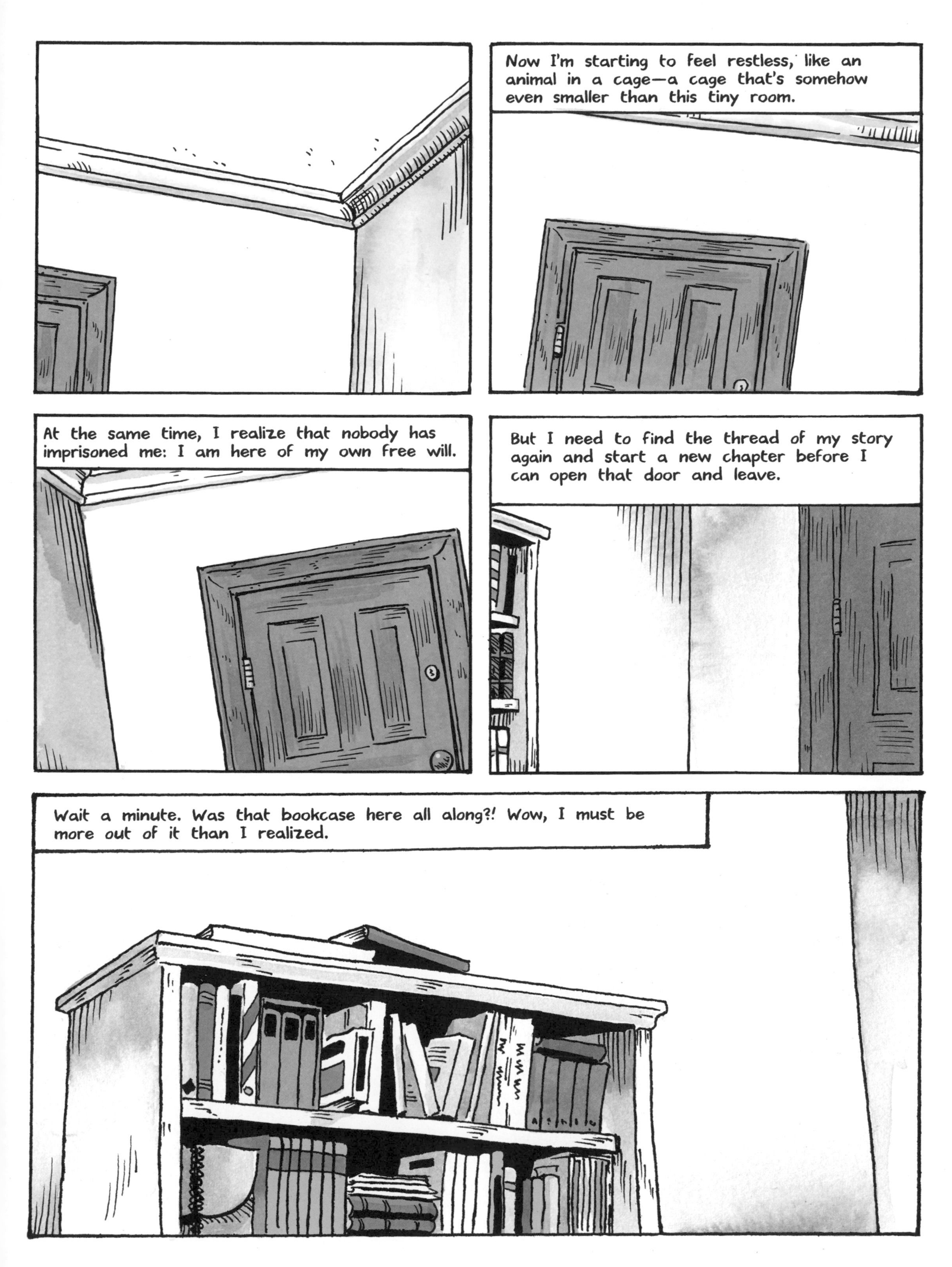
Now I'm starting to feel restless, like an animal in a cage—a cage that's somehow even smaller than this tiny room.
At the same time, I realize that nobody has imprisoned me: I am here of my own free will.
But I need to find the thread of my story again and start a new chapter before I can open that door and leave.
Wait a minute. Was that bookcase here all along?! Wow, I must be more out of it than I realized.

Has it really been there this whole time? I guess it was blocked from view by the door when I first came in...
I do remember someone calling this the "reading room."
I'm consoled by the thought of diving into books while I slowly put myself back together. It's been a long time since I've read anything.
So much potential awaits me on these shelves: I almost don't want to crack a single book.
What kind of stories will I find?
Book
Will I discover new authors?
Georges Folie's first book, Chat Noir/Chat Blanc (1913) catapulted
to fame throughout
Carribean. In this,

I take my time to examine the shape and size of the volumes on the shelves and guess their contents. I can't imagine what's in them...
Unopened, they could be anything and everything.
But I have to know: I take a first book off the shelf...
THE COMICS EXAMINER BESTSELLER
DRAWN TO EXILE
A GRAPHIC NOVEL
GAIL ESTERBROOK
And then another...
KOOKY KRITTER
THE DAILIES 1938
Well, this isn't the kind of surprise I was expecting: It turns out they're all comic books.
THE SCI-FI CLASSIC!
RED FRONTIER COMICS
VOLUME THREE
THE BEST OF
COMIX
stories
NIB COMICS

I don't think I've ever seen a whole bookcase full of comics before.

I remember those long, white cardboard boxes full of superhero comics at a cousin's house when I was a kid.

And it seems as if now everyone has a few of these "graphic novels" on their shelves— I guess they're fashionable.

But I can't say they really speak to me.

It occurs to me that I don't know whose books these are. I was assuming they had been left by the previous tenant, but maybe they belong to my landlord.

Is this the collection of someone who only reads graphic work?

Or are these things even meant for reading? Are they just collector's items?

Or else, is this the comic book "wing" of a much larger book collection spread throughout the house?

Are there other rooms devoted to science textbooks, cookbooks, or language manuals?

In any event, I'm going to be here for a while so I might as well start off with the biggest book I can find.
I look for something that will pass the time, something to take my mind off my misery...
COMICS AS A TOOL FOR LIBERATION
KOMONINO UNIVERSITY PRESS
DON'T STOP READING COMICS
TODAY OR TOMORROW
ESCAPE
YOU CANNOT
IN A ROOM WITH COMIC BOOKS
STUCK (A GRAPHIC NOVEL
YOU ARE HERE
This one's nice and heavy... and the title is appropriate.
ESCAPE
Hm, yet another comic book. Well, let's give it a try...

I'M TRYING TO FIND A WAY OUT OF THIS COMIC...
UH-OH! I'M COMPLETELY OUT OF IDEAS!
IT'S NOT IDEAS I NEED, IT'S ACTION!!
I'M SO CLEVER!
YOU THERE!
HOW DO I GET OUT OF HERE?
HERE'S A WORD YOU CAN USE—
WORDS?! I NEED ACTION!!
PLOP!
"NO WORDS," HE THOUGHT.
HE SET ABOUT MANIPULATING WHAT WAS AT HAND:
HE EXPERIMENTED WITH HITES AND BRIFFITS TO NO AVAIL. STRONG SPURLS SEEMED MOST PROMISING, BUT —
©%#*?!
PLOP!
WAIT, THE SOLUTION IS AS CLEAR AS THESE PLEWDS!!
×100
IT'S THE WORD THAT SETS US FREE AFTER ALL.
PLOP!
SO ALL I NEED TO DO IS PUT MYSELF IN POSITION...
PLOP!
AND THAT'S IT, I'M OFF.
HA HA, BYE!
PLOP!

BIFF BAM
OUCH!
OW!
WHERE AM I?
SO...
THIS CAN ONLY MEAN...
THAT I ESCAPED THE STORY...
BUT NOT THE COMIC!!
AM I DOOMED TO LIVE OUT MY DAYS IN A PARA-NARRATIVE SPATIO-TOPICAL DESERT?!
PLOP!

BOMP
OUCH!
THERE'S GOT TO BE A WAY OUT OF HERE!
PANT
PANT
HMPH!
THERE'S JUST NO END IN SIGHT!
PLOP!

BA-DONK
OW!
VOICES!
HEY! WHO GOES THERE?
THEY'RE COMING FROM BELOW.
HOW DO I GET DOWN?
?!
SQUAAAWK!
SORRY, LITTLE BIRD!
WHY, I OUGHTA-!!
SAY, WHO WERE YOU TALKING TO JUST NOW?
NOBODY.
BUT I HEARD PEOPLE TALKING.
OH, THAT'S JUST INTER-PANEL ECHO.
VOICES CARRY IN AN EMPTY COMIC LIKE THIS ONE.
PLOP! PLOP!

I wonder if anything else happens in this strange book...

The "humor" is pretty monotonous.

Maybe it shows bad faith as a reader but I'm going to skip to the end...

LOOK!
THERE'S A SIGN-POST UP AHEAD!
I HAVE A GOOD FEELING ABOUT THIS.
WHAT'S IT SAY?
...
I CAN BARELY MAKE IT OUT.
IT'S THE END!! —NO, WAIT!
"END... OF..."
IS IT THE WAY OUT?
I CAN'T TELL.
HANG ON...
DUST DUST
NNOOOOOOOOOooo!!!
PLOP!
END OF VOLUME ONE
TO BE CONTINUED

OK. That wasn't really what I was expecting from a comic book. But it gets me thinking...
hollow, heartless, mirthless, maniacal."
- The Daily Bugle
"The only real laughter comes from despair."
Does life go on after the punch line? Do the characters live on after the closing credits of a movie?
Even the most heroic character needs a reader to bring them to life, right?
BOOKS
I CANNOT HELP
(A GRAPHIK NOVEL)
And what about me, sitting here between chapters of my life... Is anyone out there reading my story?
HELP!
Is there a new chapter for me after the turn of the next page?
ESCAPE
The READING ROOM
Or am I waiting for a new book to be written?

CHAPTER TWO

It's ironic for me to seek solace in books when I consider how responsible they are for my current unhappiness.

I mean, grad school was a disaster. I slept way more than I read in that library...
phD phunnies
A CARTOON SURVEY OF COMICS DISSERTATIONS
COCONINO UNIVERSITY
KOMIX KEY NOTES
ESCAPE
READER'S GUIDE
KOMIX KEY™

School mainly taught me how to act like a Reader; how to speak and write convincingly about things I didn't really understand.
HOW TO TALK ABOUT COMICS*

It was also because of books that I met... M. (I can't even bear to write out the full name!)
And it was partly because of books that our relationship went so sour.

M.'s academic ambitions led to an ever-increasing rate of reading and writing... Maybe all that effort was a replacement for something we couldn't find together.

As M.'s career flourished, my own life floundered. M.'s published work stacked up like a wall between us. By the end I resented those books—I tore up more than a few of them.

As if that could have assuaged my jealousy. Or was it just shame at my own failure? Looking back, I realize that I never was a very serious or ambitious student...

But now, here I am in this room. I have nothing to prove and nothing to hide... maybe it isn't too late to become a true Reader. Maybe that's my task, here.

If I'm going to take this project on, I need to find a way in. Something easy that I can build on.

And I may not know much, but I should be able to handle a comic book.

Originally published in *Ontological Tales #24*, 1957.

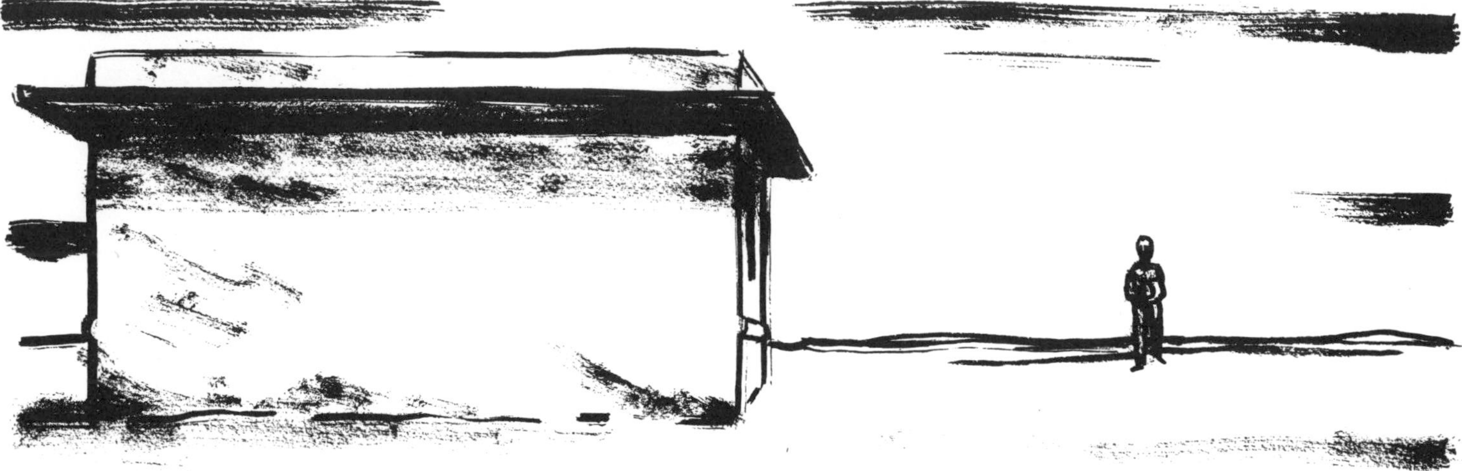

I CAN NO LONGER REMEMBER WHY I AM HERE. I MAY BE A BORDER GUARD, A RESEARCHER, A PRISONER...

AT SOME POINT I STARTED MEASURING TIME WITH A RAZOR.
I SHAVE WHEN THE STUBBLE STARTS TO OVERLAP.
OCCASIONALLY I TRIM MY HAIR. THIS LONGER INTERVAL PUNCTUATES THE SHAVING AS MONTHS USED TO BRACKET THE DAYS.

BUT NOW I HAVE GROWN USED TO THE SCANT DIET OF MY WASTELAND.

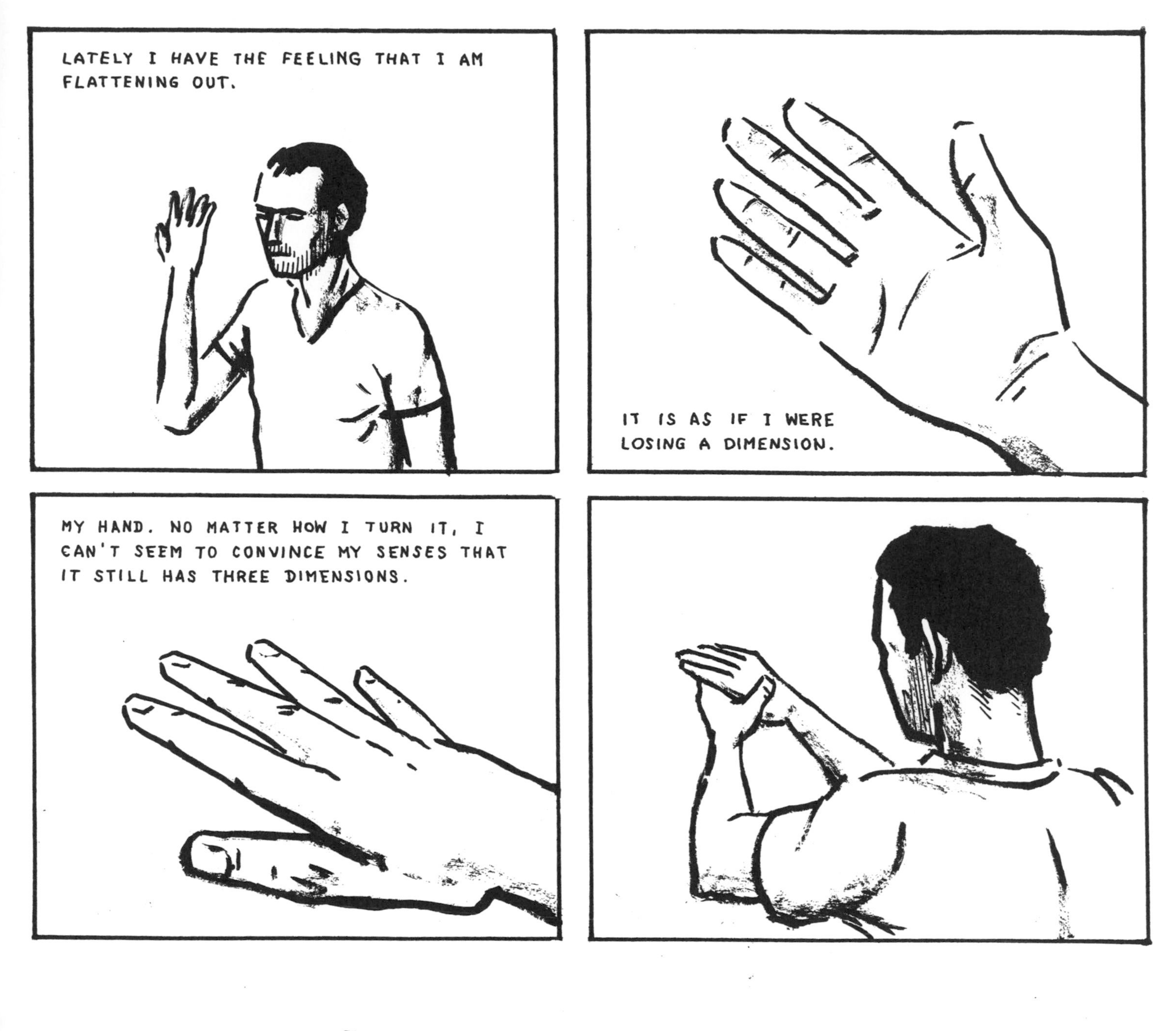
LATELY I HAVE THE FEELING THAT I AM FLATTENING OUT.
IT IS AS IF I WERE LOSING A DIMENSION.
MY HAND. NO MATTER HOW I TURN IT, I CAN'T SEEM TO CONVINCE MY SENSES THAT IT STILL HAS THREE DIMENSIONS.

I HAVE STOPPED SHAVING.

IF I PICK UP THE RAZOR AGAIN IT WILL NOT BE TO TRIM MY BEARD.

YET I DON'T FEEL THAT URGE. IN FACT I FEEL A KIND OF PEACE.
I THINK I KNOW WHAT TO DO NOW.

IF I CAN STAND HERE, JUST STAND HERE...

YES, THE TIME HAS FINALLY COME.
...OR HAS IT FINALLY GONE?

Wait... is that it? I wasn't expecting that kind of story from a "funny book." I don't get it.

It feels like a page is missing from the story. And the scenario seems pretty random to me.

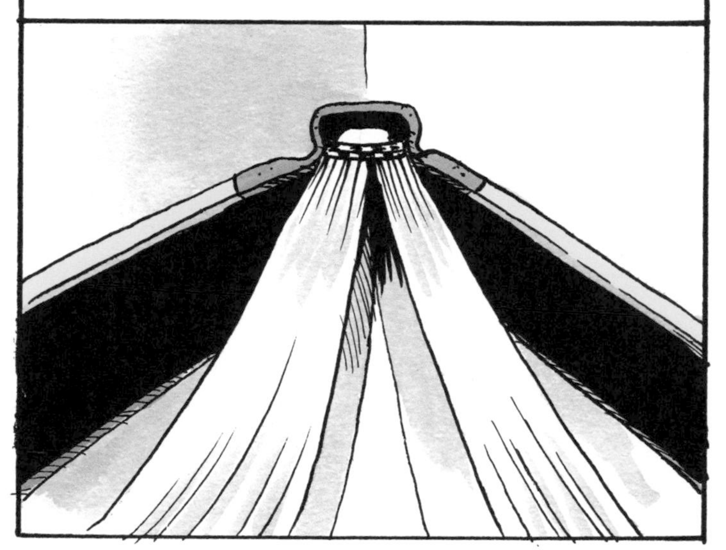
Leaving a man in the middle of the desert like that...

We never learn his name or whether he has family. He seems to have no existence outside the story.

Then again, I could ask those questions about myself: what am I doing here? How long have I been here? (I'm starting to lose track...)

I really am an idiot. I can't seem to even read a comic strip without getting confused!
That does it: even if the rest of my life is a shambles, I'm determined to learn how to read a comic book!

I'm going to need a manual or a guide to help me navigate this visual world.
I've got to find a way to decode them. I need to learn their language.
I come across what appears to be a selection of books of philosophy. Maybe they'll show me how comics work... even if they can't shed any light on my existential condition!
The Phenomenology of the Comic Book
De Comicsum Natura
How to Do Things With
Critique of Pure Comics
A Comic of On
of Comicsology
Tractatus Comico-Philosophic
to show you something remarkable!
A comic book?!
Don't judge it by its cover, I've learned something life-changing in here.
This I gotta see.
A FEW MINUTES LATER...
It's a humdinger, isn't it?
...!?!
ARE YOU TRYIN' TO TELL ME WE LIVIN' IN A COMIC BOOK?!
THAT'S WHAT DR. MARTIN'S THEORY PROPOSES.

DAT MAKES NO SENSE!! LOOK AT ME, AIN'T I FLESH AN' BLOODHOUND?!
I'M AFRAID HIS CONCLUSION IS INEXCAPABLE: YOU ARE LINES ON PAPER!! AND SO, ALAS, AM I!!
HERE'S HOW DA COMICS HYPOTHEKIS WOIKS:
DR. MARTIN POSITS THREE POSSIBLE SCENARIOS:
DA FOIST SUPPOSES THAT ALL CIVILIZATIONS GO EXTINCT BEFORE MASTERING DA AHT OF COMICS--
POOH-POOH!! ANYONE CAN MAKE A COMIC IF THEY WANT TO!!
IT'S HARDER THAN IT LOOKS, OL' PAL, IT'S HARDER THAN IT LOOKS!!
A PHILOSOPHIZIN' CAT, HUH?
BUT WAIT, IT GOES ON:
COMICS HYPOTHESIS
SCENARIO TWO SAYS THAT OF ALL CIVILIZATIONS THAT DEVELOP THE CAPABILITY TO MASTER COMICS, NONE ARE INCLINED TO DO SO.
THE COMICS HYPOTHESI
WHAT?! AND GO THROUGH LIFE WITHOUT KOOKY KRITTER SUNDAY PAGES? NO THANK YOU!
I'M AFRAID YOU'RE RIGHT, AND THAT'S PRECISELY WHAT'S SO TROUBLING, BECAUSE IT LEADS TO THE THIRD AND FINAL SCENARIO...
...WHICH STATES THAT, GIVEN THE CAPABILITY, A NON-NEGLIGIBLE NUMBER OF THESE CIVILIZATIONS WILL MASTER COMICS!!
WELL, IF THAT'S TRUE, THERE WOULD BE A PROLIFERATION OF COMICS THROUGHOUT ALL DIMENSIONS AND TIMES!!
NEW RELEASES
ESCAPE
YES, SO MANY SO THAT THERE WOULD NECESSARILY BE FAR MORE COMIC BOOK CHARACTERS IN THE UNIVERSE THAN THERE ARE CARTOONISTS...

...MAKING IT ALMOS
CERTAIN THAT WE
OURSELVES ARE
CHARACTERS IN A COMIC
BOOK AND NOT ORIGINAL
"CARTOONISTS"!!
Ya mean to say that right now I'm breathin' printer's ink instead o' factory air?
BUS
That I'm drawn
hack wearing a visor,
guzzlin' rye an rushin'
to hit a deadline?!
PHOOEY!
Suddenly I feel weirdly exposed inside my little room. I imagine a cosmic cartoonist plotting my next pratfall...
TRACTATU
What if I lived in a comic book? What kind of adventures would I have? Who would read me?
IN HIS NEW ADVENTURE,
CLINT FLICKER ASKS THE
QUESTION: "WHO ARE YOU?"
1 FLICKER
2 FLICKER
3 FLICKER
4 FLICKER
5 FLICKER
9 FLICKER
10 FLICKER
MASK
Master of Disguise
Now I'm thinking about the freedom of being a comic book character. I could try on new roles, become someone different...
A CLINT FLICKER
A CASE OF
STOLEN IDENTITY
WRENCH
IBSEN
NT FLICKER™
SIC CRIME SERIES
written by
Loren Ibsen
art by
Alan Wrench

There's a loose page tucked in the back. Is this some sort of pinup?

34
...IF YOU INSIST!
POW!
YOU ATTRACT THE M
CHARMING PEOPLE.
BOUAARFF!
PFFt. What a smug prick!
WHAT CAN I SAY? I'M A CHARMER.
OH, CLINT!
Time to celebrate having Clint Flicker out of my hair for a few months...
I can't believe I've been drawing that fascist for 32 years!
He's nothing but a thug and a bully!!
Darling, you were magnificent as always!
Why, if I ever came across him I'd—what?
Couldn't have done it without you...
YOU!! Get ready to meet your maker, you lousy—!
My dear Fellow, I think you've had a bit—
Come on, asshole, give me your best shot!
Hmmph! Well...
66%

This couldn't be meant to be part of the book, could it? It's like a poison pen letter from the artist to his character.

In any event, the spell is broken. I don't really have any interest in reading more about this Clint Flicker guy...

Never mind, there's plenty more to discover. This bookshelf has an almost endless supply of stories.

There are comics from all over the world, in all sorts of styles, to choose from.

I am dimly aware that people in Japan read a lot of comics. I've seen some pretty weird ones lying around at friends' places.

The style has always been a little off-putting to me.

But maybe I'll be pleasantly surprised. Let's take a look...

IF YOU CAN'T CONTROL THE BOOK...
I WILL BE YOUR MASTER!
BUT I WARN YOU ...
...THERE IS NO ESCAPE!!

YOU SEE, THE BOOK'S POWERS ARE GREAT...
IT IS VERY DANGEROUS!
BUT YOU WON'T ALWAYS BE SO LUCKY.
LET ME SHOW YOU WHAT I'VE LEARNED!
I AM THE ONLY TRUE READER!

AAAAAAA !!
IT WORKED!!
THE MASTER!
WE'RE SAVED!!

THE BOOK WANTS TO HELP US!
WAIT!!
THE DOOR'S LOCKED!
THERE'S NO WAY OUT!!!

Funny, I wonder if it's a bad translation, because even though it's in English I feel like I'm missing something...
20
21
22
Bukku
Bukku
Bukku
Why do all of these stories turn out to be about people who are trapped or stuck somewhere?
Arrow
COMICS
¡FORWARD!
RADICAL COMICS
1964-
HOLOGY
TURN AROUND
The library is oddly attuned to my state of mind in that way...
THE
UPLOOK PRESS
Maybe the owner of this collection is a kindred spirit, another lost soul sending me messages in bottles. Hm... Speaking of messages...
YES, EVERYONE MUST FOLLOW...
THE LEADER
UPLOOK COMICS CLASSICS
COMPLETE REPR
This book has instructions in it!
you found it!
YOU HAVE PASSED THE FIRST TEST...
go to the bottom of page 44
BEWA
LATER...
YOU WILL FOLLOW ME UP THERE!!
DON'T!! IT'S A TRAP!!
44 —
Good. Now, Find: OBEDIENCE

This is fun. I've found myself on a scavenger hunt, leapfrogging from book to book.
OBEDIENCE
HE FIRST MEMOIR IN WOODCUTS
RESIST!
MOVE ALONG
→ Hypnotic Tales issue #2, Page 13
But what's the game I've stumbled upon, here?
TALES
10¢
#2
KEEP GOING! YOU ARE UNDER MY CONTROL!
LABYRINTH OF FEAR Vol. IV p. 45
13
...And what exactly are the stakes?
FOLLOW ME NOW. WE'RE ALMOST THERE.
HE'S LYING!! DON'T DO IT!!
SHUT UP, YOU!!
AAAARGH!
45
TURN THE PAGE!!

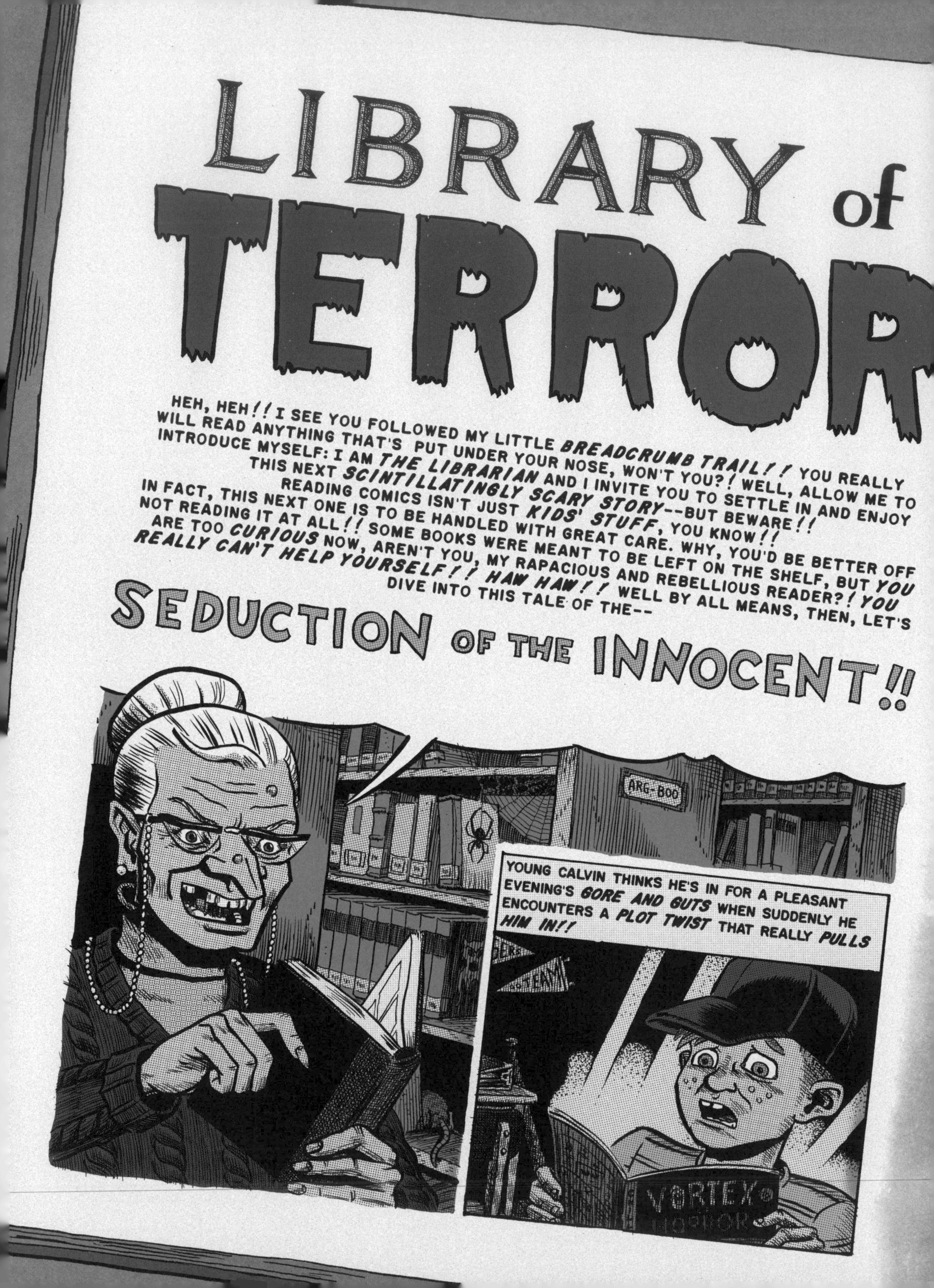
LIBRARY of TERROR
HEH, HEH!! I SEE YOU FOLLOWED MY LITTLE BREADCRUMB TRAIL!! YOU REALLY WILL READ ANYTHING THAT'S PUT UNDER YOUR NOSE, WON'T YOU?! WELL, ALLOW ME TO INTRODUCE MYSELF: I AM THE LIBRARIAN AND I INVITE YOU TO SETTLE IN AND ENJOY THIS NEXT SCINTILLATINGLY SCARY STORY--BUT BEWARE!! READING COMICS ISN'T JUST KIDS' STUFF, YOU KNOW!! IN FACT, THIS NEXT ONE IS TO BE HANDLED WITH GREAT CARE. WHY, YOU'D BE BETTER OFF NOT READING IT AT ALL!! SOME BOOKS WERE MEANT TO BE LEFT ON THE SHELF, BUT YOU ARE TOO CURIOUS NOW, AREN'T YOU, MY RAPACIOUS AND REBELLIOUS READER?! YOU REALLY CAN'T HELP YOURSELF!! HAW HAW!! WELL BY ALL MEANS, THEN, LET'S DIVE INTO THIS TALE OF THE--
SEDUCTION OF THE INNOCENT!!
ARG-BOO
YOUNG CALVIN THINKS HE'S IN FOR A PLEASANT EVENING'S GORE AND GUTS WHEN SUDDENLY HE ENCOUNTERS A PLOT TWIST THAT REALLY PULLS HIM IN!!
VORTEX
HORROR

DOWNSTAIRS, FATHER HEARS HIS BOY'S SCREAMS!! --IS THERE AN INTRUDER IN THE HOUSE?!
HE RUNS UPSTAIRS TO PROTECT HIS ONLY PROGENY!!
CALVIN?!
BUT ALL HE FINDS IN CALVIN'S ROOM IS A COMIC BOOK-- A GHOULISHLY GLOWING, PULSING PAMPHLET!!
HE PICKS IT UP TO PERUSE A PAGE OR TWO--HE REALLY SHOULD BAN THEM FROM THE HOUSEHOLD, LIKE DR. WERTHAM RECOMMENDED...
VORTEX OF HORROR
BUT THIS IS NO ORDINARY FUNNY BOOK, NO, IT'S NOT FUNNY AT ALL!!
WHAT HAPPENED?! EVERYTHING HAS GONE DARK!! FATHER FINDS HIMSELF IN A DAMP, DARK SPACE... WASN'T HE JUST READING A COMIC BOOK?!
H-HELLO?
A VOICE CALLS OUT, FAMILIAR BUT... GARBLED AND GHOULISH!!
GUHH...
GUUHH...
CALVIN!! IS THAT YOU?!
WHAT IN THE NAME...?!
A FEROCIOUS FIEND EMERGES FROM THE SHADOWS!! HAS FATHER FALLEN INTO A TRAP?
GUUHHHH!!

HIS INSTINCTS TAKE OVER--HE MUST PROTECT HIS FAMILY!! HE ATTACKS THE MONSTER WITH ALL HE HAS!!
DIE YOU DEMONIC DOG!!
FATHER IS SURPRISED BY THE FURY OF HIS OWN FLYING FISTS!!
AAARRRGH!
GUHH NOOO!! STOP, P-PLEASE!
AS THE FIGURE CRUMPLES BENEATH HIS MANLY BLOWS, FATHER REALIZES THAT THIS WAS NO MONSTER, THAT HE HAS ALMOST MURDERED HIS OWN SON WITH HIS BARE HANDS!!
C-CALVIN?!
NOOO!!
CALVIN IS HIDEOUSLY TRANS-FORMED, BUT FATHER RECOGNIZES HIS ONLY CHILD!!
GUH! D-DON'T KILL ME!!
BUT CALVIN IT'S ME -- YOUR FATHER!!
SOB!
SEEING THE TERROR IN HIS SON'S EYES HE FEELS HIS FACE AND REALIZES WITH HORROR THAT HE, TOO, HAS BEEN TURNED INTO SOME KIND OF WRETCH RIGHT OUT OF A COMIC BOOK!!
WHAT IS THIS PERNICIOUS PLACE THEY HAVE BEEN TAKEN TO?
HOW DID YOU END UP HERE, SON? WHAT IS THIS?!
I-I WAS JUST READING MY COMIC, DAD, AND IT... SUCKED ME IN!!
NOW LET'S NOT FORGET MOTHER!! SHE IS FINISHING UP TONIGHT'S CASSEROLE WHEN SHE HEARS DISTANT HOWLS OF ANGUISH. THEY SEEM TO BE COMING FROM CALVIN'S ROOM!!
SMOKE!! IS THERE A FIRE? NO!! IT'S JUST FATHER'S PIPE, BUT WHY IS IT LYING ON THE FLOOR? AND WHY IS THIS COMIC BOOK HERE, DOESN'T ANYONE ELSE CARE ABOUT KEEPING A TIDY HOME?!
BUT WAIT, WHAT IS THIS LURID LUMINESCENCE EMANATING FROM THE FOUR-COLOR FLOPPY?!
VORTEX

MEANWHILE CALVIN AND HIS FATHER STAGGER THROUGH THE DARKNESS!! THEY SEE MOVEMENT IN A LIGHT UP ABOVE !! THEY RUN TOWARDS IT!!
MAYBE IT'S THE WAY OUT!!
THEY REALIZE TOO LATE THAT IT IS MOTHER WHO IS NOW IN DANGER OF BECOMING THE NEXT VICTIM OF THIS FATAL FUNNYBOOK!!
MOMMY!! HELP US!!
DON'T READ THE BOOK, HONEY! IT'S A TRAP!!
THEY TRY TO WARN HER BUT IT'S ALL IN VAIN, SHE HAS READ THEM!!
GUUHH!!
GNN!! ARGH!!
BEFORE SHE CAN REACT, CALVIN'S MOMMA FINDS HERSELF IRRESISTIBLY DRAWN TO THESE LINES ON PAPER!!
MOTHER FINDS HERSELF IN A DARK, DAMP PLACE. SHE IS CONFUSED, TERRIFIED!! SHE HEARS SOME GHOULISH GROANS, THEY SEEM TO BE COMING CLOSER!!
WH-WHERE AM I?!
GUUHHHH!!
SHE SENSES TWO FIGURES WALKING TOWARDS HER -- MONSTERS!! SHE FEELS AN URGE TO DEFEND HERSELF! A BRUTAL INSTINCT KICKS IN...
SHE ATTACKS FEROCIOUSLY!! IT FEELS... GOOD!! SHE DOESN'T STOP TO THINK ABOUT WHO SHE MIGHT BE ATTACKING, SHE JUST WANTS BLOOD!!
AS SHE DEVOURS THE RAW MEAT OF HER OWN LOVED ONES, A FAINT WHIFF OF BURNING CASSEROLE FILLS THE PAGE...
AND WHATEVER BECAME OF THAT AWFUL BOOK, YOU ASK? WHY... IT'S THE COMIC YOU'RE READING RIGHT NOW!! PUT IT DOWN QUICK OR YOU TOO WILL END UP LOST IN A FUNNYBOOK!! HAW HAW!! BUT MAYBE THAT'S WHAT YOU WANT!! I THINK YOU'D LIKE TO BE SWALLOWED UP BY A BOOK, WOULDN'T YOU?!
OTHERWISE, HOW WILL YOU EVER GET OUT OF THAT ROOM YOU'RE HOLED UP IN?! YES, I'M TALKING TO YOU, DEAR READER, SITTING THERE LOCKED UP IN YOUR LITTLE ROOM, HAW HAW!!

Wait, was she really talking directly to me?!
LABYRINTH of FEAR
VOLUME 4
AAAHAHAHAHAHA
NO!
I'm confused... Is this some kind of prank?
FEATURING
THE LIBRARIAN
But... how could anyone plan this?
HEE HEE HEE
LIBRARIAN
The room is spinning...
HA HA
HAW
THE
It's impossible... I must be reading into things!
FEAR
HAW! HAW!

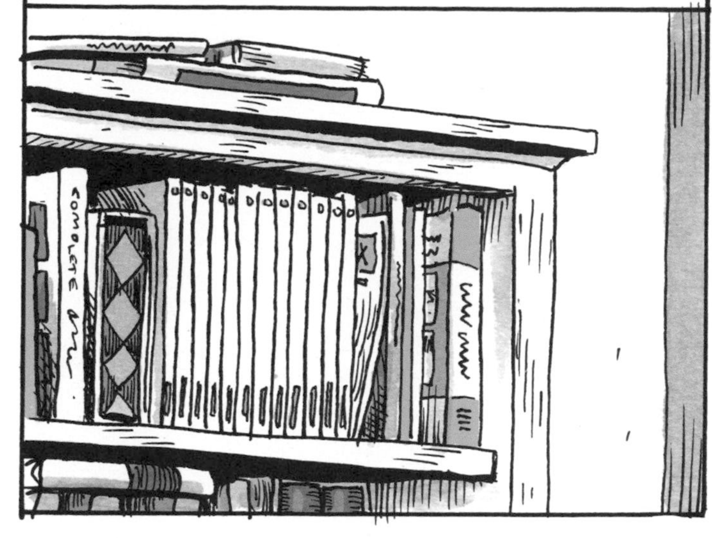
I feel like I'm caught in a waking dream... I can't manage to remember who suggested this room to me, now.

Are these books meant for me, alone, to read?

Is this some bizarre plot of my landlord's? Does he get his kicks by driving tenants slowly insane with paranoia?

This bookcase is beginning to seem more and more like a menacing puzzle box to me.

CHAPTER THREE

I'm starting to believe drawings have a greater power than words to get under your skin...
HAW! HAW!
I'm definitely letting my imagination run wild by reading all these horror and crime stories.
LABYRIN
FEAR
AAAAHAHAHAH
No!
I look for something more sober to read, something grounded.
ECONOMICS OF GLOBAL COMICS PUBLISHING Volume 5
$
¥
€
I need something that talks about real life, about everyday experiences...
BETTER LIVING through COMICS
A "graphic novel"—Yes, that's the kind of book I need right now!
DOUBLE SOLITAIRE
GRAPHIC NOVEL SELECTION READING CLUB

CANTINA
Rent's past due.
So pay it then.
No way! I paid the electric bill last week.
I'm low on cash, I need you to pitch in.

...
We could throw a rent party.
Yeah? Who we gonna invite? Nobody wants to hang out with us since you groped Ann at Marcy's picnic!
Fuck that, you're the one who made a pass at Charles at Tim's party!
As if he would take you between your meds and the weight you're putting on...
Sorry, I...
We're out of beer.

Yeah, OK, I get the idea... People are unhappy in love. We get stuck with people we can't stand yet we don't have the power to leave them. Right, check.
I know the story. After all, that's why I stuck with M. for such a long time.
It's not like that.
at porn all
Thinking about it now, the situation was so obviously terrible. Especially as it wore on...
kept the baby...
Oh, come
can't blam
on me
Strange, the layout of the apartment really reminds me of our old place... we had the same wall nook echoing the rounded doorway, and there was that hat someone left on our fridge...
Too many memories! I came here to recover, not to linger on past disasters...
Maybe what I need is something really corny... some kitschy romance.
THRO
3
4
5
6
7
2
THROBBING HEARTS
THE COMPLETE COLLECTION
I LOVED... A MODERNIST!!

NOBODY HAD BOUGHT HIS PAINTINGS AND IT TURNED HIM BITTER.

NOBODY UNDERSTANDS MY WORK... WELL, TOO BAD FOR THEM!!

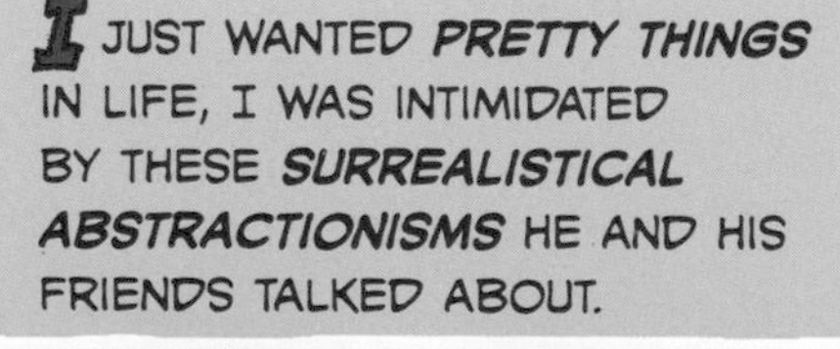

I COULDN'T **HELP** MYSELF, THE PILLS MADE ME FEEL BETTER, THEY MADE ME **FORGET**... ALMOST...

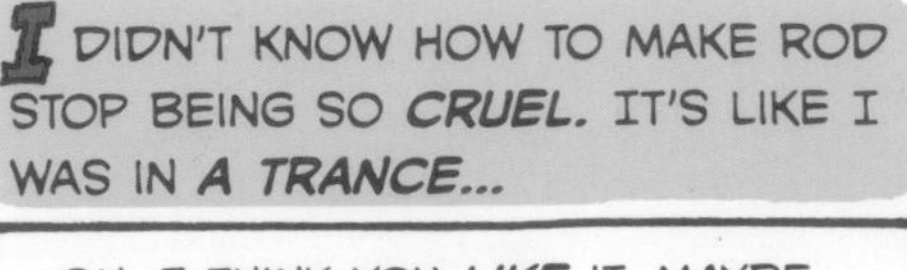

I DIDN'T KNOW HOW TO MAKE ROD STOP BEING SO **CRUEL.** IT'S LIKE I WAS IN **A TRANCE...**

THE WEEKS THAT FOLLOWED WERE **A BLUR...** ROD TREATED ME LIKE A PLAYTHING, **A SLAVE...**

THE **HUMILIATION** WAS **UNBEARABLE!!** I HAD REACHED MY **LIMIT!!**

THESE **PILLS** I WAS TAKING, IF I TOOK **ENOUGH** I COULD **END** IT.

BUT THEN I REALIZED... WHY SHOULD *I* BE THE ONE TO GO?

THE **SOLUTION** TO MY PROBLEMS WAS **CLEAR:** I PREPARED **A LETHAL CONCOCTION** AND BROUGHT IT TO **ROD** IN HIS STUDIO...

For a tacky soap opera, that is a surprisingly accurate portrait of the last stage of my time with M. Although, to be honest, the roles don't always line up with my particular experience...

Ugh! I rifle through books at random, trying to find something to change things up.

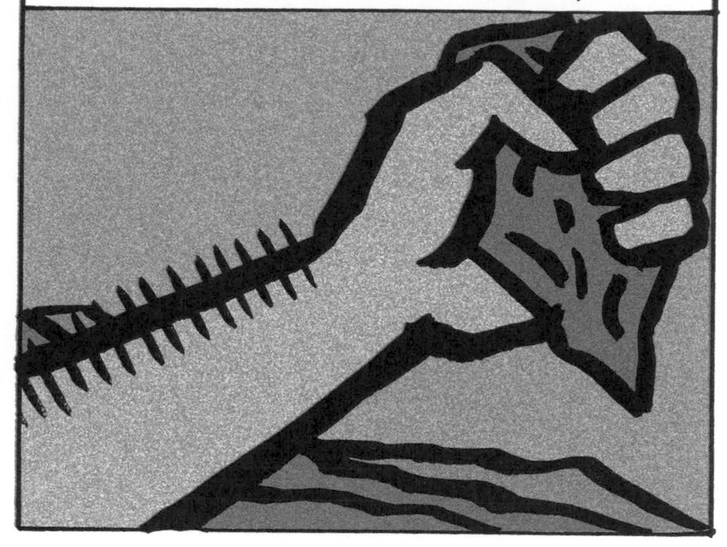

But it seems like every comic book I look at ends up directing me back to my own failures in some uncanny detail or other.

I'm probably reading into things. We always look for ourselves in stories, don't we? But all this has nothing to do with me.

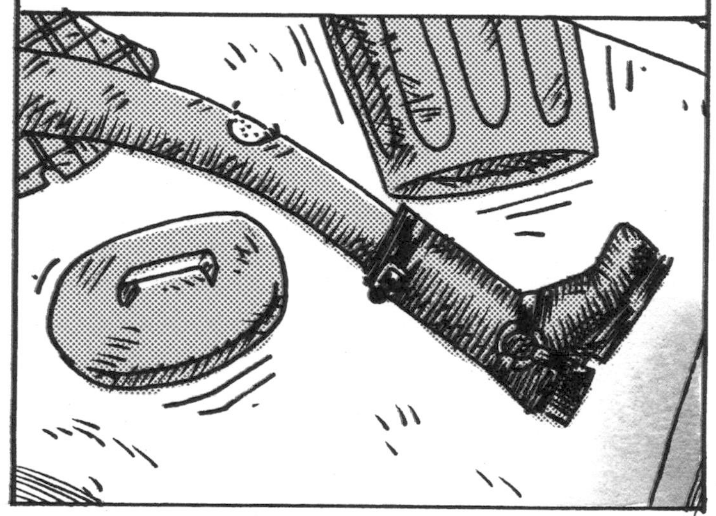

I've got to stop beating myself up! I mean, reading is just a way to pass the time. I am looking for a distraction, nothing more.

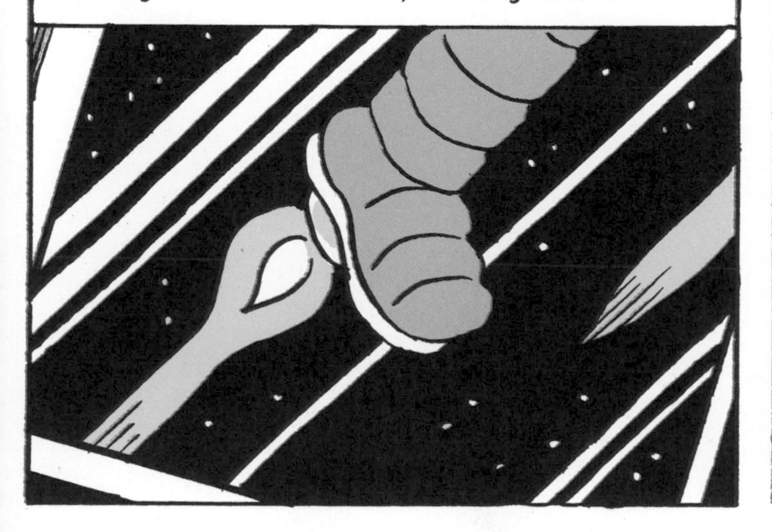

How about a superhero comic? That's sure to be completely simple and escapist, right? The exact opposite of my pathetic life...

THOUGHT YOU WOULD HAVE MORE *PAGES* IN YOUR LAST *CHAPTER*, DIDN'T YOU, *BOOK-WORM?!*
IT'S NOT TOO LATE TO CHANGE, *PAPERCUTTER*. YOU CAN SET ME FREE NOW AND WE CAN END THIS.
OH, WE SHALL *END* THIS, ALL RIGHT.
YOU *SENT ME AWAY* ALL THOSE YEARS AGO, AND NOW IT'S *MY* TURN TO THROW THE *BOOK* AT YOU!!
URK
HAHAHAHA!!

AND BY THE WAY, I'M NOT PAPERCUTTER ANYMORE! CALL ME: SHREDDER!!
I KNOW WHERE YOU CAME FROM ... PAPERCUTTER. I PULLED YOU OUT OF THAT GUTTER. I HELPED YOU ONCE ... AND I CAN DO IT AGAIN... I CAN FORGIVE YOU...
I DON'T WANT TO BE FORGIVEN!! YOU SHOULD BE BEGGING ME FOR FORGIVENESS!!
IT'S TIME TO SQUISH YOU, PAPER PEST!!
HAHAHAHA!!
GET OUT OF MY LIFE, YOU WORM, YOU WORM, YOU WORM!!
What?!

Did... did he really just say that?!

Could M. have somehow planted this library here to torment me? To push me over the edge?

Who was it again that told me about this room? Why can't I remember anymore?

Am I in a coma, lying in a hospital bed somewhere? I can't help feeling like none of this is real, like I'm going to wake up soon.

Or am I suffering from some kind of psychotic break? Are these messages I left for myself, warnings or reminders? Is a saner version of myself trying to guide me back to sanity?

Up until now I've been avoiding the bottle in my bag but right now I need some relief...

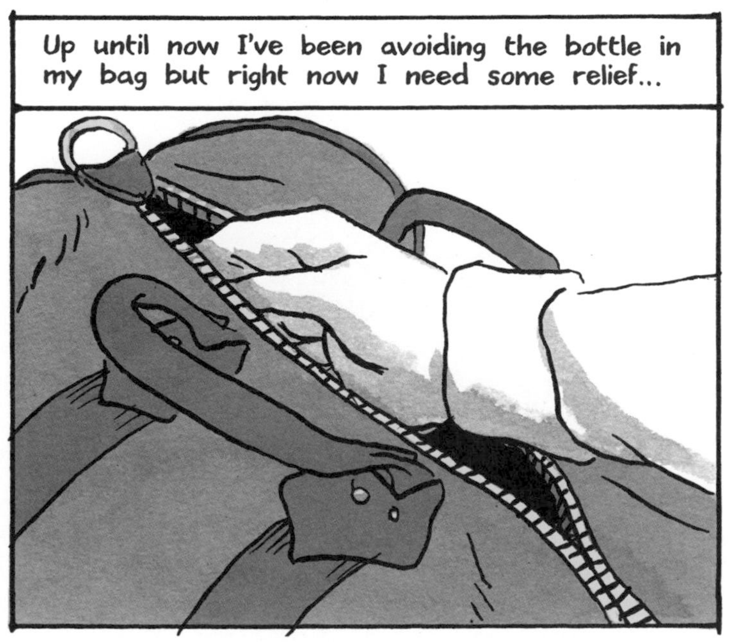

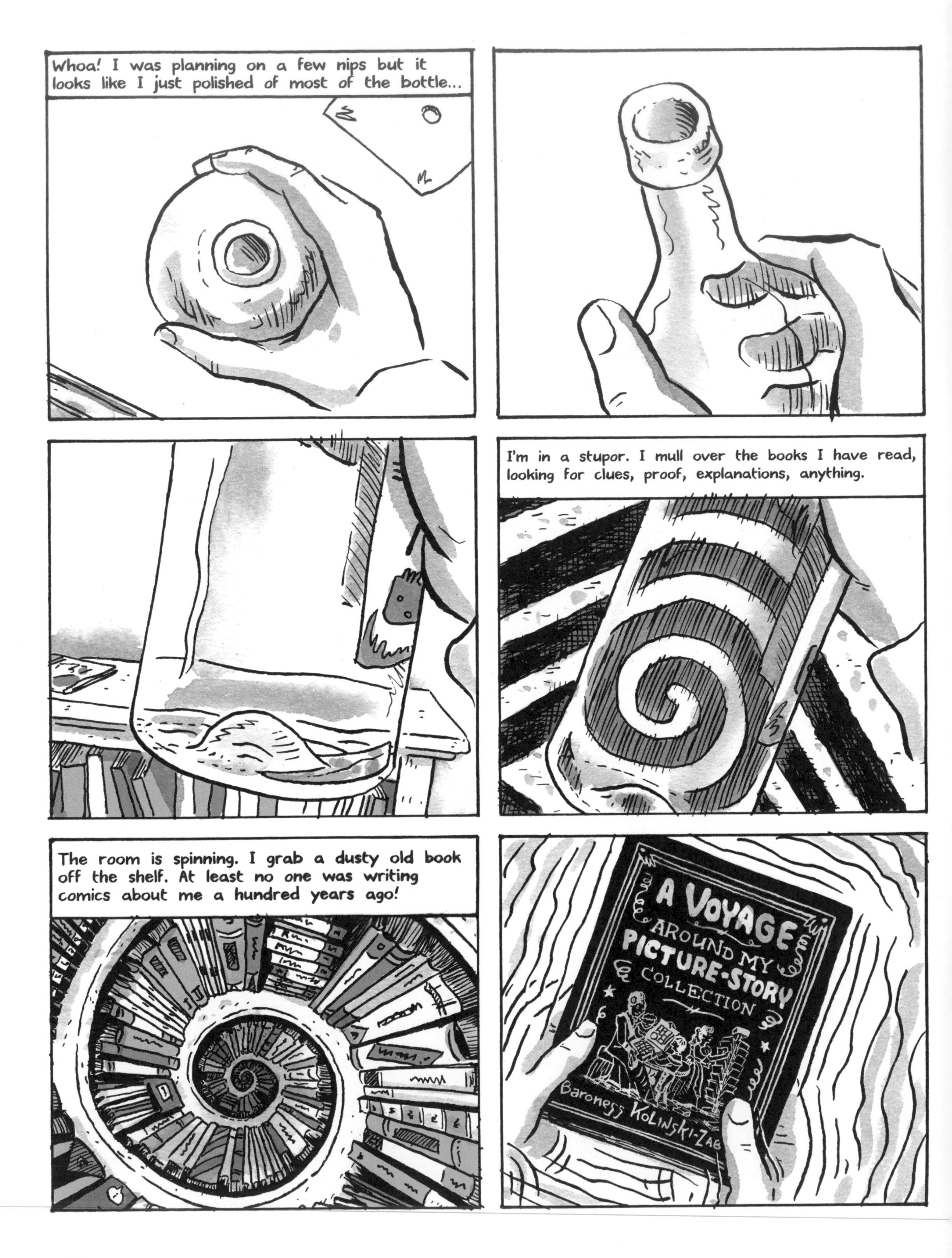
Whoa! I was planning on a few nips but it looks like I just polished of most of the bottle...
I'm in a stupor. I mull over the books I have read, looking for clues, proof, explanations, anything.
The room is spinning. I grab a dusty old book off the shelf. At least no one was writing comics about me a hundred years ago!
A VOYAGE AROUND MY PICTURE-STORY COLLECTION
Baroness Kolinski-Zab

Welcome, friend reader! I would like to share with you a few books from my 'picture-strip' collection.
That's what I call this new style of book I have been collecting. Whenever I pass a book merchant or a bouquiniste, I cannot resist the compulsion to purchase a tome or two.
A proper noble woman like myself is expected to have dainty hobbies but I have become besotted with this new picture-word hybrid.
You see, in these books, the authors do not merely write stories, they also illustrate them with choice views and vistas, portraying expressions both facial and gestural which convey sentiments language can only inchoately hint at. In some cases words are dispensed with entirely — to no great detriment to the sense of the work as a whole!
This baloone is too shoddie
This is my fynest stoffe
I prefere this one
I can fully immerse myself in the lived experience of characters in situations very different from my own. Allow me to share with you a few examples.
Let us start by perusing this little booklet I cherish particularly, an account of life on a distant island. We live with a family and observe their rituals and traditions...

I can almost taste this stew of orange beans and beach piglet, can't you?
Oh, my, this is most unfortunate!
We've opened to the part where the White Men come and abduct the father into bondage!
You see, this book is in fact the memoir of the enslaved islander, drawn years later on his deathbed!
He never made it home again— and if we're not careful, neither shall we!
Ah, but wait, what's this?!
Ah, yes, this was the next book I wanted to shew you!

It's a very different sort of book, not at all based in reality as far as I can tell, it's more like a dark fairy tale...
We're in a cold northern land. It's damp, we draw our shawl closer but still the dampness chills us.
From out of the gloom, a figure of a woman approaches across the moor...
She unsettles us... We flee from her!
The master of this decaying mansion is even more terrifying!
I think I'd rather live on the moor with that ghost than be a member of his household!
To the kitchen, the only place where we'll find some warmth!

Ah, much better, but we don't have much time: the master will be here soon to try to have his way with this darling girl.
Too bad he doesn't know that the chef is waiting with her cleaver!
It's all quite sordid, you see, the "ghost" on the moor is in fact the master's half-sister... It's dreadfully complicated. When they were younger, he—
Well, I think it's best we move on the the next book.
Now this one is peculiar.
IT TAKES PLACE ON ANOTHER WORLD, IN FACT, IT'S OUR OWN MOON!
THE STORY IS SET FAR IN THE FUTURE...
HUMANS HAVE COLONIZED THE MOON, EXPLOITING THE MOON-GIRLS TO MINE PRECIOUS LUNAR DIAMONDS WHICH FUND AN ENDLESS WAR BACK ON EARTH!

BUT THE MOON-GIRLS HAVE BRED A DIAMOND-ENCRUSTED MOON-YETI TO EXTRACT REVENGE!
I'M AFRAID I OPENED TO THE WRONG PAGE... WE'RE IN THE LAIR OF THE MOON-YETI!
GGRRRRRR
WE NEED TO GET OUT OF HERE FAST, SHE'S INDISCRIMINATE IN HER SLAUGHTER, AS WE WILL LEARN LATER IN THE BOOK!
RRROOAAA
I REMEMBER! THE MOON-GIRLS HAVE A SECRET HATCH, IT'S SOMEWHERE OVER... HERE!
RROOAAAAOOO
NOW, I BELIEVE THEY WILL HAVE JUST FINISHED THEIR ESCAPE-DIRIGIBLE. WE'LL BE SAFE THERE.
I DO APOLOGIZE FOR THE DARK TURN MANY OF MY BOOKS SEEM TO TAKE!
But that's the nature of my taste... Because in the end, isn't it a bit more exciting when there are thrills and chills?
MY FATHER WANTED ME TO READ MORE SOBER BOOKS AND I DO READ THOSE KINDS, TOO.
yet I find myself ever drawn to strange tales and locations.

BOOKS ARE A WAY FOR ME TO ESCAPE – NO, BETTER: TO LIVE MORE LIVES THAN JUST MY OWN.
POSZT
Now, I have a final book I want to share with you, it's the most precious book in my library.
Without it I feel I wouldn't be able to exist at all!
On the surface, there is nothing unusual when you start to read it.
But come with me, I want to show you something.
We need to be very quiet, now.
Take a look around, what do you see as your eyes get used to the darkness?
Yes, a bookshelf! A secret library hidden deep within my book collection!
And next to it a pallet, on which a figure sleeps restlessly.

Huh?!
TEQUIL
EL AXOLO

Did I fall asleep? Am I in a nightmare? Am I conscious now or do I need to read one more book to be able to wake up?

I'm struggling to focus... I can't think clearly. I shouldn't have drunk all that tequila!

This has to all be in my mind! Or am I in the middle of a complete psychological breakdown?

But don't they say that if you're truly crazy, you won't believe it? And if that's true, I can't be insane...

But then, that would mean that all these hidden messages and threats are real!! I feel sick... The room fills with black ink...

CHAPTER FOUR

I must have passed out. For how long, I don't know. I need to force myself awake.

All these voices are crowding in on me... Whoever is doing this, I can't let them get away with it. I need to clear my head!

I've had it. I can't take any more of this. There has to be a way to get out of this situation! But, how? I'm so exhausted...

I'm awake but hungover... Huh? What's this on the futon? Did I pull it out last night? Or did someone leave it there for me to find? I hardly dare open it...
At the same time, I need to do something... I don't know what the solution is but all I've got right now is these books.

I take a deep breath, brace myself, and start, once more, to read...
LA MULATA DE CÓRDOBA

The island prison of
San Juan de las Viñetas
Gulf of Mexico, 16th Century
We keep her here...

La mulata de Córdoba...
She is beautiful and she never ages.
She helps the lovesick and the poor.
She fornicates with Satan!
Tomorrow she will be judged by the Holy Office of the Inquisition.
Guard, give me a piece of coal!

Guard! Come see!
Guard, what's missing from this boat?
Ha ha, only that it should sail away!
Well...

... it shall.

He's gone mad.
sail away...
sail away...

Finally, a story about an escape.
Leyendas de la Colonia
LA MULATA DE CÓRDOBA
Leyendas de la Colonia
LA MULATA DE CÓRDOBA
The woman appears to be a witch of some sort.
She draws those magical symbols on the sails of the boat...
Then she climbs right into the drawing and escapes her prison.
I wish I had a guard to ask for some charcoal.

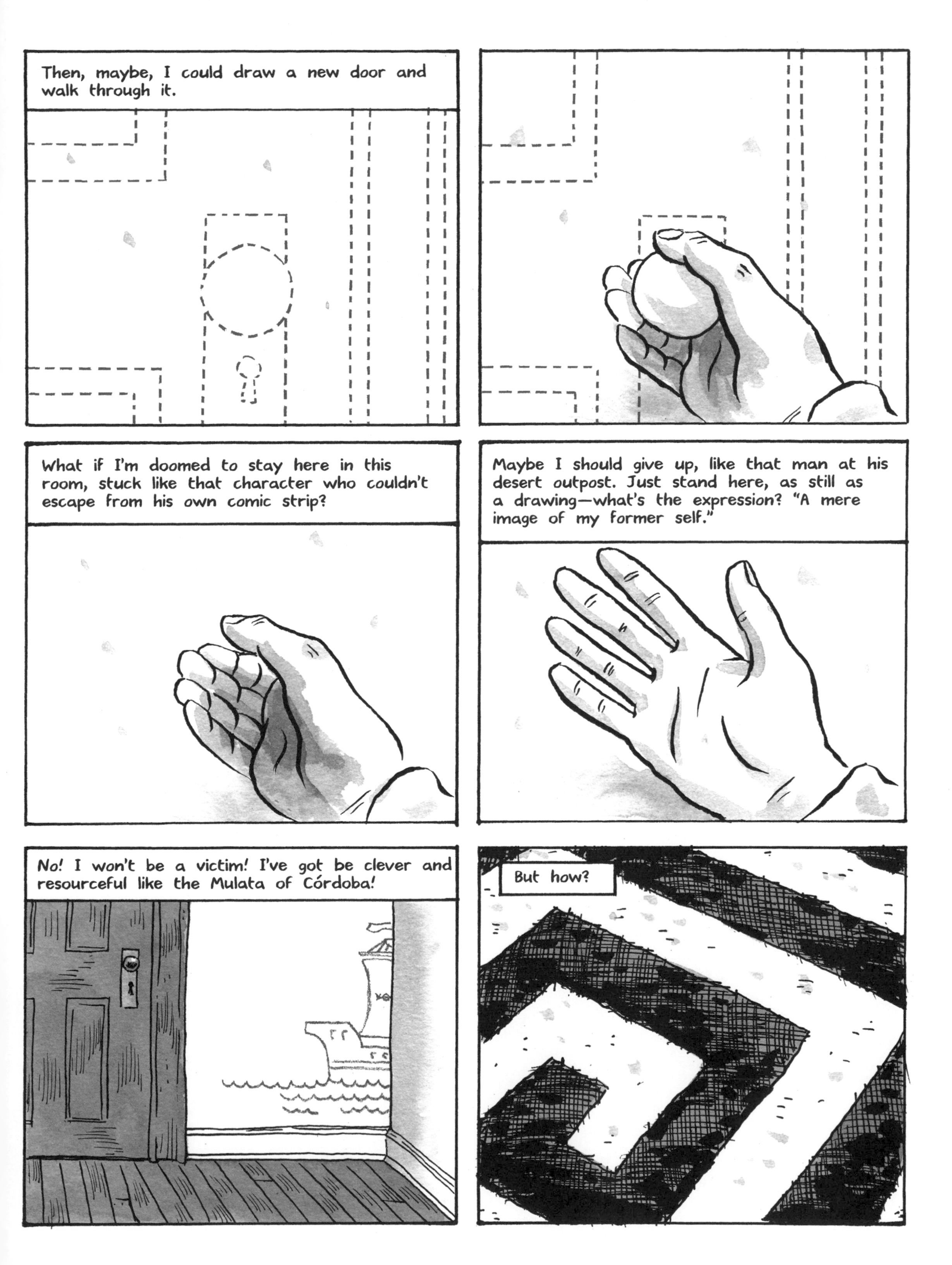
Then, maybe, I could draw a new door and walk through it.
What if I'm doomed to stay here in this room, stuck like that character who couldn't escape from his own comic strip?
Maybe I should give up, like that man at his desert outpost. Just stand here, as still as a drawing—what's the expression? "A mere image of my former self."
No! I won't be a victim! I've got be clever and resourceful like the Mulata of Córdoba!
But how?

Going back to the bookcase, a sort of notebook catches my eye. I haven't noticed it earlier.

It appears to be somebody's sketchbook.

No name or date... As I examine it, something slips out of the spiral binding.

There are several pages of comics inside, completely drawn but with no text in the word... bubbles or whatever they're called...

Maybe if I write some dialogue, I can take some control over the narrative.

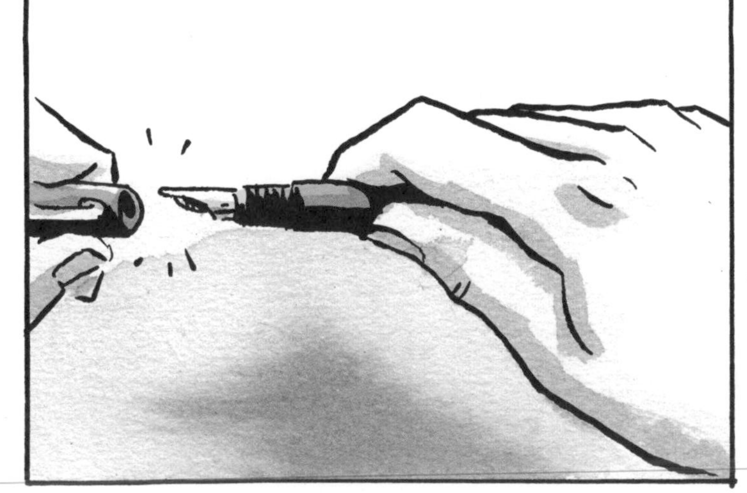

I don't know what's going on so I just write whatever comes to mind.
Who am I?
ARR
HARDW
The hero, I guess.
And I seem to be headed somewhere in particular.
Hey! Is this lettering awful?
Yep.
Is this better?
Letter more slowly, treat it like you're drawing the words.
Yeah, I'm getting the hang of it. Thanks!

The comic book hero marches down the city street with determined steps... Hm, I guess that's redundant... some writer I am!
Hi, I'm a kid, I don't know why I'm in this comic!
I think this guy's going to murder us!
As the children flee, it occurs to me that they might be right about this guy!!
Bogey Man...
Killer, rapist.

He's pretty creepy... Hang on, this looks a lot like the house I'm staying in...
I'm getting ready to murder someone!!
He's walking toward the door of the room I'm renting!
My god... Who drew this? And why?!
I'm starting to get really freaked out, here.

KNOCK KNOCK
My stomach knots up. Is it my imagination or did someone really just knock on the door?! I don't dare answer. I sit still.
I pick up the sketchbook again. There's nothing on the next page. The rest is blank.
An idea occurs to me: maybe if I can draw the rest of the story, I'll find a way out!
I have no idea how to draw but I have now been reading these comic books for what seems like weeks (months?) straight.
I pray to La Mulata and uncap the pen once more.

I know where to start: That scary character is knocking at the door. But who's on the other side?
KNOCK KNOCK
Well, why not make myself into the hero of the story? Or the victim or whatever!
But how will I draw myself? I've never been much of an artist...
I could aim for an accurate likeness but that would be impossible...
I could draw myself any way I wanted to, after all. I could even draw myself as a man.
Let's see, it seems to me that the drawing in the comics I've been reading tends to be pretty simple... And maybe a bit idealized...
Voilà.

OK, a quick review of the pages and I am ready to begin...
For the sake of drama, I try to draw my reaction as nervous and apprehensive.
KNOCK KNOCK
Who's there?
What do you want from me?!
Open the door!
No!

Open it now... and let me in!
Open the door and no harm will come to you!!

Wait...

Why am I letting myself be intimidated and threatened in my own comic?!

I'm the one holding the pen, here.
I'm so tired of letting outside forces determine my narrative.

I don't need to play the victim. I control the story now.

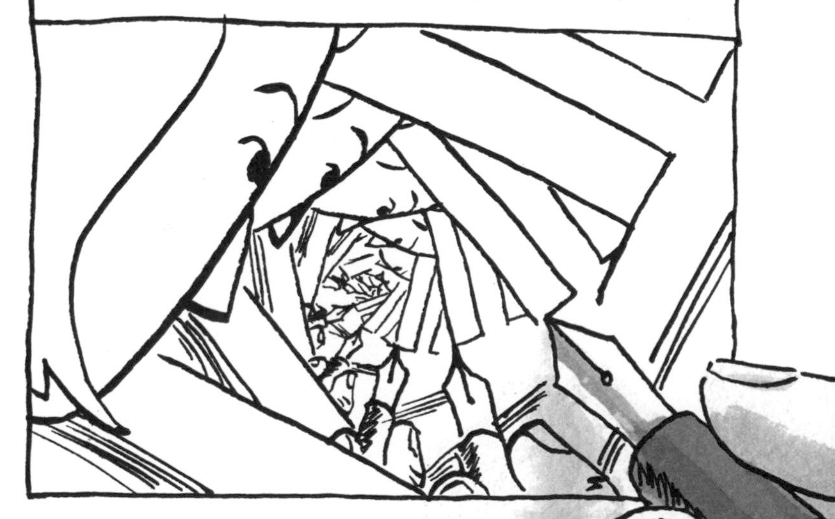
And, yeah, maybe there's another me drawing me, drawing me... But I can say for sure that right now I'm the one creating this story!

And all these books... They're mine, now. They'll do my bidding, as if I created them myself. Just watch this...
ANA
MORPHOSIS
LET'S GO!!
ALL ABO
It's time to leave!
NEXT STOP, WILLOUGHBY..
WAYOUT
COMIX
THE BEST-SELLING SAGA REACHES ITS THRILLING CONCLUSION!
You're right, it's true: you can leave now.

Finally, I understand. There really is nothing to fear. The pieces fall into place, the puzzle suddenly and surprisingly reaches its solution.

I'm not a character in someone else's story any more.

I can leave my failures behind in this room. M. is powerless over me. My past fades like a vague memory from a book read long ago.

There's one last thing to do. I grab the pen and I turn to go.

It's time to start over, I'm going to take my line for a walk and see where it takes me.

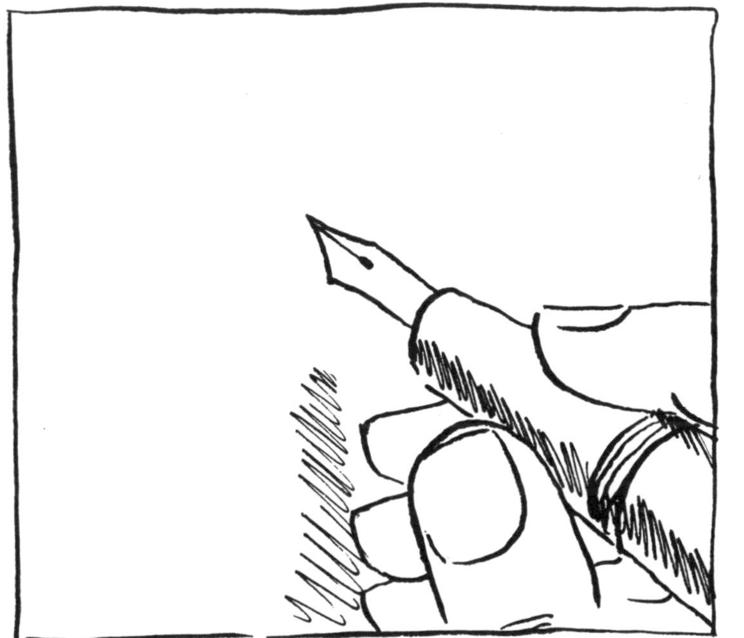

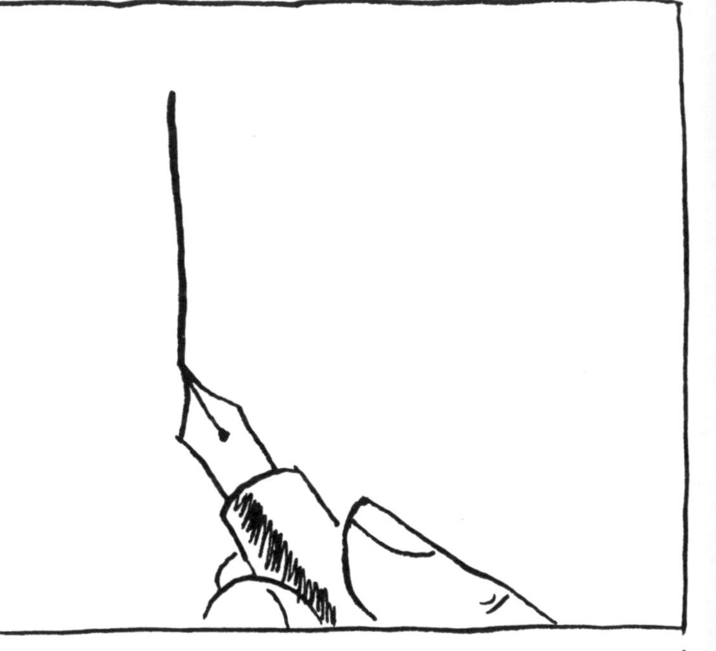

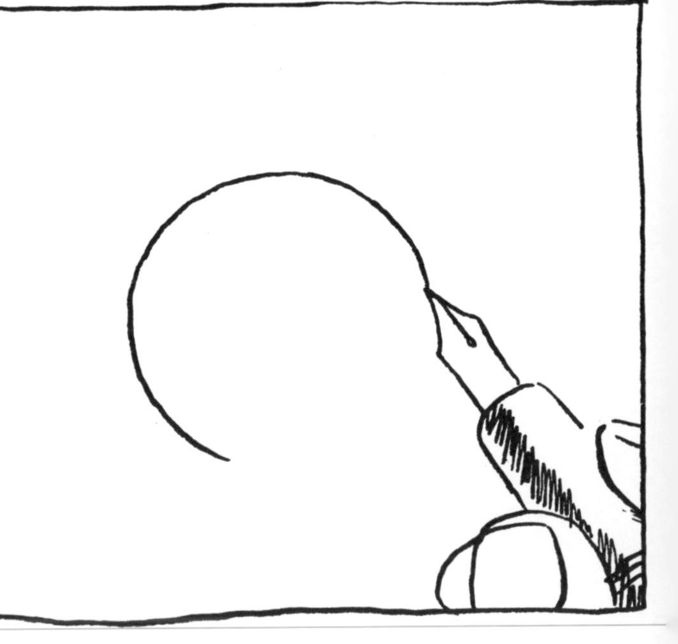

CLICK!

Now my pen draws me into the future. I don't know what stories I'll tell outside this room but I am ready to face the blank page.
CLICK!

EPILOGUE

KLIK!
THE ROOM IS SMALLER THAN I EXPECTED, BUT IT WILL DO FOR NOW.
ANYWAY I DON'T HAVE ANY OTHER OPTIONS. AND THE THING I NEED RIGHT NOW IS SOME TIME TO MYSELF.
FLOP!
THE PREVIOUS BOARDER SEEMS TO HAVE LEFT A LOT OF BOOKS BEHIND.
I LOOK THROUGH THEM, HOPING TO FIND A NOVEL TO PASS THE TIME.
FUNNY THING, THOUGH...
CAPE
IT TURNS OUT THAT THEY ARE ALL COMIC BOOKS.
EX LIBRIS

ACKNOWLEDGEMENTS

I worked on portions of this book during a residency at La Maison des Auteurs in Angoulême, France, as well as at the Atlantic Center for the Arts in New Smyrna Beach, Florida.

I'd like to thank Casey Burns for the Leroy Lettering font and Blambot for the HometownHero and SilverAge fonts.

Many people encouraged, advised, and inspired me while I worked on this book. I'd particularly like to thank: Marc-Antoine Mathieu, Grégoire Seguin, Étienne Lécroart, François Ayroles, Justin Wadlow, Pili Muñoz, Italo Calvino, Julio Cortázar, Josh O'Neill and Maëlle Doliveux, Tom and Gina at Partners & Son, Derek Beaulieu, Don Madden & Tom Kaczynski, and my apologies to anyone I have—inevitably—forgotten to include.

Extra special thanks for their thoughtful and crucial feedback to: Jessica Abel, Tom Hart, Josh O'Neill, Jason Little, Aldara Madden, and Jasper Abel.

Dedicated to Sally Madden, the original and greatest Reader in my life.